For you girls

I SURVIVED

THE ERUPTION OF MOUNT ST. HELENS, 1980

by Lauren Tarshis

illustrated by Scott Dawson

Scholastic Inc.

Text copyright © 2016 by Lauren Tarshis
Illustrations copyright © 2016 by Scholastic Inc.
Photo of Mount St. Helens on page iv © Robert Krimmel/
U.S. Geological Survey

ISBN 978-0-545-65852-2

10 9 8 7 6 5 4 3   16 17 18 19 20

Printed in the U.S.A.   40
First printing, September 2016
Designed by Yaffa Jaskoll
Series design by Tim Hall

CHAPTER 1

SUNDAY, MAY 18, 1980
8:32 A.M.
MOUNT ST. HELENS, WASHINGTON STATE

For more than 100 years, Mount St. Helens had been quiet, a beautiful mountain surrounded by forests. Hikers climbed its winding trails. Skiers raced down its snowy slopes. Children splashed in its crystal clear lakes.

Except this peaceful mountain was not a mountain.

It was a dangerous volcano, a deadly cone filled

1

with molten rock and poisonous gases. And soon it would explode with the power of ten million tons of dynamite.

In the minutes before the eruption, eleven-year-old Jessie Marlowe and her best friends Eddie and Sam were in a forest near St. Helens. The day was warm and bright, the sky brilliant blue. St. Helens rose up over them, its perfect triangle peak sparkling with snow.

And then,

Kaboom!

Suddenly, Jess was in the middle of the deadliest volcanic eruption in American history.

She watched in horror as the sky turned pitch-black. A blizzard of ash poured down, swirling up her nose and making it almost impossible to breathe. Hot rocks pelted her like bullets shooting down from the sky.

Then, *whoosh*, a blast of wind exploded out of the mountain, a white-hot mix of ash and gas and shards of rock. It raced down the mountain at jet speeds, burning everything in its path. The heat hit Jess and the boys, knocking them down.

2

Jess felt as though she would burst into flames. Every breath was like inhaling fire.

But the terror was just beginning.

The eruption had shattered the mountain, and now a fifty-mile-wide avalanche of rock and mud and melted ice was taking aim at the valley below. It grew larger by the second. It snatched up trees and boulders. It tore away bridges and swept away houses.

It would destroy everything — and everyone — in its path.

CHAPTER 2

EIGHT WEEKS EARLIER
SUNDAY, MARCH 23, 1980
SPIRIT LAKE MEMORIAL HIGHWAY,
WASHINGTON STATE

"Skeleton Woman is not real," Jess said.

"She's totally made up," Sam agreed.

"Can we please stop talking about Skeleton Woman?" said Eddie, Sam's twin brother. "You're giving me the creeps."

It was Sunday morning, and Jess and the Rowan twins were riding in the back of a red

4

Ford pickup truck. Mr. Rowan, the twins' dad, was up front, singing loudly along to his favorite disco song.

They were about twenty miles from their hometown of Cedar, Washington, rumbling along a winding highway. The road was lined with trees, a forever stretch of forest and rolling hills.

They were heading to the Rowans' fishing cabin, which was on Loomis Lake, up closer to Mount St. Helens. It wasn't fishing season quite yet. But Mr. Rowan wanted to get the cabin ready. He was happy to have Jess and the twins tagging along for the day.

Looking across at the twins, Jess saw two matching buzz-cut heads, four identical green eyes, and about ten thousand freckles. When they were little, Jess would have done anything to look more like them. She'd blown out her birthday candles with a wish for green eyes instead of brown. She'd even drawn Magic Marker freckles onto her pale skin.

But Jess had outgrown that. And anyway, the twins weren't so exactly alike. Eddie was quiet and serious. Sam never shut up and he had a fearless streak that sometimes got all three of them into big trouble.

Like today, for example.

Mr. Rowan didn't know the real reason that Jess and the boys wanted to get up to the mountain: Skeleton Woman.

She was an evil woman from a scary old story, kind of like the witch from Hansel and Gretel, but worse, because she supposedly lived around here. She had wild white hair and coal-black eyes and rusted metal claws instead of fingers.

According to the old legend, she lurked in the dark forests that covered the slopes of St. Helens, the mountain that rose up over this whole valley. She wandered through the woods, searching for children, whose bones she used to make her magic powders.

It was just a creepy story, the kind you told while you were roasting marshmallows or huddled together at a slumber party. But some of the kids in their school actually believed Skeleton Woman was real.

One girl, Missy Samuels, swore Skeleton Woman lived in a broken-down shack in the woods near Loomis Lake.

"That whole part of the forest is cursed," Missy had said, flicking one of her curls. It had been last Wednesday, and they were on the blacktop at school. Eddie had been impatiently bouncing a red rubber ball. Usually they played kickball at recess, but Missy wouldn't stop yakking about Skeleton Woman.

Jess used to be good pals with Missy. But that was about a million years ago, before Missy's dad got an important new job at the lumber company. Now Missy lived in the biggest house in Cedar — the *only* big house in Cedar.

"Skeleton Woman is in those woods," Missy went on. "My dad says some of his workers saw her. And now they refuse to step foot in that part of the forest."

"That's not true," Jess said.

"They saw her, Jess!" Missy insisted. "Her clothes were covered with blood!"

"It's just a dumb story," Eddie scoffed.

"If you're so sure, maybe you should go to the shack yourselves," Missy said.

This was starting to sound like a dare.

"Fine," Sam blurted out. "We'll go."

Jess and Eddie had shared a look that meant *Please tape Sam's mouth shut now!*

Too late.

"Fine," Missy said. "You better bring a camera, because I'll need proof."

Within minutes, she'd blabbed to everyone, making it sound like a big joke — with Jess and the twins as the punch line.

So of course they couldn't back out.

Which is why they were here, on this cold morning, sitting in the back of the red pickup.

"But what if she's actually there?" Eddie asked.

"Then Jess will take her picture," Sam said.

Jess gripped her backpack, where she'd put Dad's camera. She felt a pang of guilt. The camera had been Dad's prized possession, and Jess knew that Mom wouldn't want Jess taking it into the woods. But Jess would be extra careful. She'd even wrapped it in a plastic bag, in case it rained.

"How will I take her picture?" Jess asked.

"Mrs. Skeleton Woman," Sam said in a high voice, "say cheese!"

Eddie leaned forward and bared his teeth like a skeleton.

"Cheese!" he growled. A glob of egg glistened on one of his teeth.

They all burst out laughing, and Jess's honking giggle mixed with the twins' loud snorts. It took them all a few minutes to calm down.

Eddie's face got serious again.

"You guys aren't scared, are you?" he asked.

"Nah," Sam said.

"No way," Jess lied.

Of course they were scared. Who knew what they would find in that shack? Even if they didn't find Skeleton Woman and her bones, there could be a bear, or a thousand rats. Jess shuddered.

But fear was better than other feelings, wasn't it?

Like missing her dad, who died in a car accident two years ago.

Or worrying about Mom, who seemed so lonely and worked way too hard.

Those sad thoughts were always flickering at the edges of Jess's mind.

So it was good to have other things to think about, like an evil old witch with smoldering black eyes.

CHAPTER 3

They pulled into the parking lot at the lake and Mr. Rowan came around to open the tailgate.

"Hello, troops," he boomed.

With his big belly, bushy beard, and laughing eyes, Mr. Rowan had always reminded Jess of a younger version of Santa Claus. Mrs. Rowan was half his size, and about twice as strict. They all loved her, of course. Mrs. Rowan was Jess's mom's best friend. But today the boys didn't seem too upset that their no-nonsense mom wasn't here to keep them in line. Mrs. Rowan was away for the week. She was taking care of the twins' grandma who lived about fifty miles from Cedar.

There were only two other cars in the parking lot today, a beat-up Toyota and a white pickup. There was an older woman standing by the truck. Even from a distance, they could see her long gray braid and bright smile.

"Hello!" she called out with a wave. "What a day!"

"You said it!" Mr. Rowan exclaimed.

It was usually pouring rain around here in late March. But this morning the sky was bright blue and the sun shined down.

"And just look at our pretty mountain," Mr. Rowan said, putting an arm around each of the boys and smiling up at St. Helens.

The mountain's lower slopes were blanketed with green trees. The top was covered with snow. Its perfect triangle peak sparkled in the sun. Jess always felt a flash of pride when she looked at St. Helens. No, it wasn't as famous as Mount Hood, across the border in Oregon. And it wasn't as tall as Mount Rainier, which loomed over Seattle, about two hundred miles to the north of Cedar. But folks who lived here knew St. Helens was the most beautiful mountain in the Cascade Range. And if most people had never heard of it, who cared?

Mr. Rowan gathered his supplies and headed to his fishing cabin.

"I'll be organizing my gear," he called. "Don't go far. And, Jess, keep those boys out of trouble."

"Will do!" Jess promised.

Jess and the twins watched him disappear down the little path that led to the cabin.

"This is going to be fun," Sam said, rubbing his hands together.

"Fun?" Eddie said.

"Let's face it," Jess said. "We have nothing better to do."

The twins nodded.

Cedar wasn't a terrible place, but it sure was dull. Only about four hundred people lived there. The closest grocery store was twenty miles away. Last weekend the big excitement was the elk that wandered onto Main Street and blocked traffic for an hour.

But Jess and the twins had their mountain and their forests.

And they had each other.

Eddie held out his hand, palm up. Jess and Sam laid theirs on top of his. It was a three-way secret handshake they'd made up back in kindergarten.

"All for one," Sam said.

"And one for all," Jess and Eddie chorused.

Dad had taught them that saying a long time ago. It was from *The Three Musketeers*, which

was a book way before it became the name of a candy bar. The book was about three best friends who'd do anything for each other.

Like Jess and the twins.

They linked arms and started marching toward the dark woods.

"Watch out, Skeleton Woman!" Sam screamed. "We're coming to get you!"

CHAPTER 4

Missy had said the shack was about half a mile up the winding trail above the lake. They figured it would take about thirty minutes to get there.

The twins walked slightly ahead. Right away, they started bickering about who was the best pitcher on the Seattle Mariners. The baseball team was only three years old, and it wasn't very good. But the boys had become instant fans. Their dream was to see a home game in person. But they'd never been to Seattle. Neither had Jess. Missy had gone there last month for her birthday. She'd come back bragging about eating at a fancy steak restaurant. And of course she'd seen a Mariners game. The twins hated hearing about that!

Soon they'd crossed over into the best part of the forest, with old trees that soared up so high it seemed they were touching the sky. Jess breathed in the spicy smell of the pines. Her ponytail swung in the chilly breeze. Her mind drifted, and the twins' bickering voices faded. She walked with light steps, whispering the names of every tree and flower, careful not to trample any saplings or mushrooms as she stepped.

It was how Dad had taught her to be in the forest.

He'd loved it here so much. He and Mom and Jess had come up here whenever they could sneak away from the little diner they owned in Cedar. They'd camp under the trees and hike the trails. Dad would stop every minute to photograph Mom or Jess or some bird perched on a branch. He'd saved up for two years to buy his camera, and his dream had been for one of his photographs to be shown at a gallery in Seattle.

No, he'd never taken a photography class. He'd never worked anyplace other than their diner.

But you never knew.

"Anything's possible," Dad always said.

And the way he looked at Jess, his eyes bright with hope, she didn't doubt it.

Maybe he'd gotten his optimism from his granddad Clive Marlowe.

Clive had come here to southern Washington State when he was just sixteen, to work as a lumberjack. Back then there were no highways or restaurants or towns in the Cascades. There were still wolves in the woods, and grizzly bears that stood ten feet tall.

But mainly there were trees — some of the most spectacular trees on Earth. The oldest ones had been here before George Washington was born, before the *Mayflower* sailed, when the only people here were Native Americans quietly hunting and fishing among the trees.

But that all changed in the 1800s when American settlers came. They chased away most of the native people. Lumber companies bought up the forests.

They sent men like Clive in to cut down the trees. Soon enough, most of those centuries-old trees had been chopped into wood to build ships and railroads and buildings for America's brand-new cities.

Lumberjacking was dangerous. The biggest trees weighed fifty tons, as much as a traincar. They came crashing down with so much force that the earth shook a mile away. Men were crushed by falling branches. They lost feet and hands to the blades of axes. Clive himself was almost blinded by a spray of razor-sharp wood chips.

But it wasn't the danger that got to Clive. It was watching those big trees disappear. He grew to hate the grinding sound of saws and axes. He dreaded the moment when a tree started to fall over, how its wood would moan and creak as though it was crying out in agony.

So he quit work at the lumber company and opened a diner he named Clive's. Folks were sure the diner would fail. But Clive didn't listen.

And fifty years later, Clive's Diner was still there, passed down through the proud Marlowe

family like a priceless treasure. Dad had taken it over after his own dad passed. And he and Mom ran it together until Dad's car accident two years ago.

After Dad died, Mom wasn't so sure she wanted to stay in Cedar. She'd always dreamed of becoming a teacher, of living in a city like Seattle.

But how could she close the diner that had been in Dad's family for generations? And how could they leave Cedar, where every crack in the sidewalk reminded them of Dad?

Sometimes it felt like Mom and Jess were as rooted here as the old trees.

Thinking about all of this made Jess feel dizzy, as if she was teetering at the edge of a cliff.

But then Sam's voice jolted her back.

"There it is!" he cried.

Jess looked ahead.

It was the shack.

It sat there in the distance, as though it had been waiting for them.

CHAPTER 5

"Yikes," Eddie muttered.

The small cabin looked like nobody had stepped foot inside in years. The porch sagged, the windows were boarded up, and the chimney had crumbled to bits. Thick, twisting vines crawled up the sides. It was easy to imagine two deadly eyes peering through the cracks in the wood. Jess could practically hear a croaking voice whispering to her.

Give me your bones!

Jess's muscles twitched. All she wanted was to get away from here.

But then she pictured Missy's smirk.

Don't be a dope, Jess told herself.

There was no such thing as Skeleton Woman. But all-too-real Missy would be waiting for them at school on Monday morning.

Jess gathered her courage and stepped forward.

Sam and Eddie glued themselves to her side.

Together they moved through the tangled brush, pushing through the thorny bushes that grabbed at their clothes.

Skeleton Woman is not real. Skeleton Woman is not real.

Jess said these words over and over to herself.

But just to be safe, she scanned the ground for traps. She remembered that detail from the old legend — how Skeleton Woman dug big pits in the ground to trap her victims. The holes were as deep as graves. She'd cover the pits with branches and leaves and wait for helpless victims to tumble to their doom.

Skeleton Woman is not real. Skeleton Woman is not real.

Sam reached for the door first and gave it a little push.

Creak!

The door swung open. Jess braced herself for a hideous scream, for two rusty-clawed hands to reach out and pull her into the darkness.

But wait . . . it didn't look so scary. A buttery ray of sunlight beamed through a crack in the roof. There was a battered table and chair and some cardboard boxes of junk. A paintbrush and a can splattered with red paint sat on a shelf.

There were no baskets of bones, no cauldrons of bubbling witches' brew.

It was just an abandoned hunting shack, like hundreds of others that dotted the forests around here.

They all stepped inside and looked around.

"So hurry up and take the picture," Eddie said.

"Okay," Jess said, shrugging off her backpack. She opened it up and took the big black camera out of its plastic bag. The sight of it sent a little jab through her heart; it reminded her so much of Dad.

She put her pack on the floor and lifted the camera, aiming it at the room.

But then a strange noise filled the shack.

Rrrrrrrrrrrrrrrrr!

The hairs on the back of Jess's neck stood up straight.

"What was that?"

Her whole body started to shake. Her teeth rattled.

But it wasn't her fear that was making her shake. The whole cabin was vibrating. The walls trembled and the floor rolled up and down under their feet. Jess staggered and fell to her knees. Dad's camera slipped from her hands and flew across the floor.

What was happening?

Skeleton Woman is not real. Skeleton Woman is not real.

But if it wasn't Skeleton Woman, who — or what — was it?

"It's the curse!" Sam screamed.

CHAPTER 6

They stumbled out of the cabin. But the shaking was outside, too.

The ground bucked up and down. The trees swayed back and forth violently.

Jess and the boys clung to each other for balance as they staggered to the trail. But then *crash!* a huge tree fell right in front of them.

They turned to escape in the other direction, but *crash!* a massive limb hit the ground just feet from where they stood.

They had to get out of there!

"Wait! My dad's camera!" Jess shouted.

But there was no going back.

The ground was now splitting apart, like ice breaking on a frozen pond. Clods of dirt flew up. Yawning holes opened in the earth, some deeper than any grave.

Jess and the twins huddled close together, their heads ducked down low, their arms wrapped tight around each other. More tree limbs crashed to the ground.

Jess braced herself for the crushing blow of a huge branch hitting her head.

And then, in a blink, the shaking stopped.

The forest went mute.

The only sounds were their own sobbing breaths.

They stood there too shocked and scared to speak.

And then, without a word, they joined hands and ran down the trail.

They jumped over fallen branches and holes in the ground, over roots and rocks. Jess kept looking over her shoulder, sure that Skeleton Woman was after them. She could practically feel the witch's oven breath huffing at her back. Missy had been right all along: This forest was cursed!

They were almost to the parking lot when they heard Mr. Rowan shouting for them.

He came rushing up the trail, moving his burly body way faster than Jess ever thought he could.

He grabbed all three of them in a bear hug.

They hadn't yet caught their breath when a man came hurrying up to them. He had dark brown skin and curly hair and looked to be about Mom's age.

"Hey! Are you all okay?"

Jess and the twins peeled themselves away from Mr. Rowan.

"We're all in one piece!" Mr. Rowan called out. "You?"

"I'm fine," the man said, dusting off his pants. "That was a pretty strong quake."

"Sure was," Mr. Rowan answered.

Jess and the twins stared at each other in shock — and relief.

An earthquake. Of course!

Earthquakes happened sometimes in Washington State. They even had earthquake drills at school. They'd been so brainwashed by Missy's dumb story that they weren't thinking clearly.

Mr. Rowan introduced himself to the man.

"Skip Rowan," he said.

"Tim Morales," the man said, shaking Mr. Rowan's hand and smiling warmly at the twins and Jess.

"Do you have a cabin here, Tim?" Mr. Rowan asked.

"Actually, I'm here for work," he said, reaching into his shirt pocket and taking out a business card, which he handed to Mr. Rowan.

"*Dr. Timothy Morales,*" Mr. Rowan read, "*Department of Seismology, University of Washington.* You study earthquakes? Well, you came to the right place today."

Dr. Morales nodded. "Actually we've detected at least fifty mild earthquakes in this area, all in this past week. They're coming from directly under St. Helens. At first we weren't sure what these earthquakes meant. But now we're certain they're warning signs."

"Warning of what?" Mr. Rowan asked.

Dr. Morales was quiet for a moment. And then he looked up at St. Helens.

And what he said next was more unbelievable than any horror story Jess had ever heard.

"I think Mount St. Helens is about to erupt."

CHAPTER 7

SIXTY MINUTES LATER
CLIVE'S DINER
CEDAR, WASHINGTON

Jess and the twins and Mr. Rowan walked through the front door of Clive's. Mom took one look at them and nearly dropped the coconut cake she was carrying. Jess knew they must look bad, streaked with dirt and covered with scratches from their run down the mountain.

"What on earth?" Mom cried, putting the cake on the counter and hurrying over to them.

Mom listened with wide eyes as they told her about the quake. She wrapped her arms around Jess and hugged her tight. Jess opened her mouth ready to tell her about Dad's camera. But then Mr. Rowan announced the big news.

"We heard that St. Helens might erupt."

Mom stared at him in shock.

"That's ridiculous," she said. "Who would say such a thing?"

A voice from the end of the counter called out.

"I would."

Mom had been so busy fussing over Jess and the twins that she hadn't noticed Dr. Morales, who'd walked in behind them. Mr. Rowan had invited him to join everyone at Clive's, and he'd followed them down the highway in his car — that beat-up Toyota they'd spotted in the parking lot. Turned out that living through an earthquake made people fast friends.

"Tim here is a volcano expert," Mr. Rowan said. "He works at a lab in Seattle."

Mom looked Dr. Morales up and down with surprise. "You're a scientist?"

With his overgrown curls and faded jeans, Dr. Morales looked more like a singer in a rock band than a person who worked in a laboratory.

"I'm not wearing my scientist uniform today." Dr. Morales laughed. "But yes. I've been studying St. Helens for the past eight years."

Mom sent Jess and the twins to get cleaned up. When they returned, they found Mom and the men sitting in a booth. There were mugs of hot chocolate waiting for Jess and the boys. There were no other customers in the diner, so Mom was free to sit with them.

"But I didn't think St. Helens could erupt," Mom said.

"I didn't either," Mr. Rowan said. "I figured it was the kind of volcano that's dead, or whatever that word is . . ."

"You mean *extinct*," Dr. Morales said. "But no. St. Helens is not extinct. It's just been dormant, which means it's been quiet."

"But it's always been so peaceful," Mom said.

"It has been perfectly quiet, for one hundred and twenty-three years," Dr. Morales said. "The last time it erupted was in 1857. But St. Helens is the most active volcano in the West. It has erupted dozens of times over the past few thousand years. There have been massive explosions, lava flows, avalanches, and mudslides. One eruption about five hundred years ago buried much of the valley under about two hundred feet of rock and ash and mud."

"What about Cedar?" Mom asked.

"Cedar is up on a ridge. And I don't think any of the eruptions have reached this far. It's a safe place."

"Good," Mom said with a nervous smile. "I was about to start packing up."

"Amazing that nobody around here knows about all this," Mr. Rowan said, shaking his head.

"Actually, people did know," Dr. Morales said. "Native Americans had been living here in the Cascades for about seven thousand years before the American settlers arrived. They knew St. Helens was dangerous and stayed away from it. They wouldn't even fish from the lakes on the mountain. The Cowlitz tribe called this mountain Lawetlat'la. It means 'mountain of fire.'"

The words seemed to hang in the air.

"What's the most dangerous part of an eruption?" Mom asked.

"Lava?" said Sam, with just a little too much excitement.

"Lava is dangerous," said Mr. Morales. "But around here, the bigger dangers are mudslides and rock avalanches. And I worry about the pyroclastic surge. That's a wave of hot air that explodes out of the volcano. It's truly devastating. That's what happened in the eruption of Mount Pelée."

"Never heard of Mount Pelée," Mr. Rowan said.

None of them had.

"What happened?" Eddie asked.

"I don't know if you want to hear about that," Dr. Morales said. "It's a grim story."

"We do! We do!" Sam begged.

"Go ahead," Mom said.

And so, as the hot chocolates grew cold, Dr. Morales told the story of the deadliest volcanic eruption in the twentieth century.

CHAPTER 8

"The year was 1902, on the Caribbean island of Martinique," Dr. Morales began. "The island's capital is the city of Saint-Pierre, which is is right on the Caribbean Sea. And it sits right at the base of Mount Pelée.

"Pelée was a fairy-tale kind of mountain, with bright green slopes covered with trees."

Like St. Helens, Jess thought.

"Few people realized that it was actually a volcano. It had rumbled a few times over the centuries. But it had been silent for more than fifty years.

"And then, in April of 1902, Pelée woke up. All through that month, there were hundreds of very small earthquakes."

"Like the ones today?" Eddie asked.

Dr. Morales nodded.

"There was also the strong smell of sulfur gas seeping from deep inside the Earth. That gas builds up as a volcano is becoming more active, and it can leak out of the Earth. It has a horrific smell, like rotten eggs. Around Pelée, the stench became so strong that people fainted in the streets. Horses collapsed.

"But few had any idea that the quakes and the sulfur were warning signs that Pelée was going to erupt. The science of volcanoes was unknown back then. People simply didn't understand that they were in danger.

"That changed in early May, when a small eruption sent ash and glowing rocks into the air. A few days later, part of the volcano broke away, and a river of boiling mud and ash roared down the mountain at eighty miles an hour."

"That's faster than my truck," Mr. Rowan said.

"Some mudslides can travel even faster. That one killed more than one hundred and fifty people." Dr. Morales said.

He looked at Jess and the twins.

"The story gets more grisly. Maybe I should stop here."

"No!" Sam shouted. For him, this was even better than a Mariners game.

Dr. Morales looked at Mom, who nodded.

"Okay," he said. "Because next come the snakes."

"Snakes?" Mom said.

"The earthquakes disturbed thousands of snakes that had been living on the mountain. They came slithering down into Saint-Pierre. Some of them were venomous six-foot-long pit vipers. Hundreds of people died from bites."

"Goodness, I'm going to have nightmares about this," Mom said.

"Sorry," Dr. Morales said. "I'm getting carried away. I should stop."

But no way would Sam let him.

"It's all right," Mom said. "You might as well tell us how this ends."

"I think we can take it," Mr. Rowan agreed.

"So at this point, people were terrified, as you can imagine," Dr. Morales continued. "Many people left by ship. But most couldn't afford to flee, or had no place to go. And the leaders of Saint-Pierre kept telling people the worst was over."

"I'm guessing they were wrong," Mom said with a cringe.

"Very wrong," Dr. Morales said.

"The real disaster happened on May 8, a cloud of sulfur blanketed the city. First there was a massive explosion. Pumice and mud rained down. And then a wave of searing hot gas and ash exploded out of the mountain and into Saint-Pierre."

Dr. Morales took a breath.

"Within seconds, thirty thousand people were dead."

Jess gasped. And the boys' chins practically hit the table.

"Thirty thousand people?" Mom said slowly. "How is that even possible?"

"That was the pyroclastic surge. Imagine the wind in a hurricane, but with air that's scalding hot. Then add toxic gas and ground-up rock and ash. The heat is so extreme that it burns everything in its path. People died instantly, without even knowing what happened to them."

Nobody spoke for a moment, and even Sam looked queasy. The only sound was the gurgle of the soda fountain.

"And you're saying that the same thing could happen here?" Mom asked.

Dr. Morales nodded. "It could. But luckily, there aren't thirty thousand people living right at the base of St. Helens."

That was true. The mountain was surrounded by forests, with just a few towns dotting the valley.

A chill came over Jess, even though she was warm and snug sitting between the twins.

For her entire life, St. Helens had been the beautiful mountain rising into the sky. She'd grown up hiking its winding trails, diving into its cold lakes, and fishing for trout in its streams. Just looking at St. Helens out her window made her feel calm, as if it were watching over her somehow.

Okay, maybe somewhere in the back of her mind she'd known that St. Helens was a volcano. Everyone around here knew that. But Jess never imagined that it was a *real* volcano, a killer that could explode.

"When do you think this eruption is going to happen?" Mom asked.

Dr. Morales shook his head.

"It's hard to say for sure. But I do believe it's going to erupt violently. And I think it's going to happen soon."

CHAPTER 9

Jess couldn't sleep.

Every time she closed her eyes, she imagined St. Helens exploding, and then a flaming wind sweeping down the mountain.

Finally she took her quilt and went into Mom's room.

Mom was awake, too, and moved over in bed to make space for Jess.

"Don't be worried," Mom said. "You heard what Dr. Morales said. We're safe here in Cedar."

"I know, but I just can't stop thinking about it."

"I can't, either," Mom said. "But I think we need to put it out of our minds. Maybe Dr. Morales has just watched too many disaster movies."

Jess smiled. "That part about the snakes was a bit much."

Mom giggled a little.

"But do you really think St. Helens is going to erupt?" Jess asked. "Could that actually happen?"

Mom turned toward Jess.

She moved closer, so their noses were almost touching.

"Whatever happens, you and I will make it through. Like we always have, and like we always will."

Mom said the words without a shred of doubt.

Jess looked at Mom. She still needed to tell her about the camera.

But suddenly Jess was so tired.

She closed her eyes. And with Mom's calming words whispering through her mind, Jess fell asleep.

The next morning, Jess and Mom had barely finished breakfast when the twins came barging through their door.

"We're in the newspaper!" Sam cried.

"You are?" Jess said with surprise.

"Not us," Eddie cried. "St. Helens!"

They held up the Seattle paper, with a headline screaming out from the front page.

MOUNT ST. HELENS AWAKES!

Jess couldn't believe that their mountain was on the front page of an important newspaper like the *Times*.

At school that day, their teacher, Mr. Daley, canceled their fractions quiz. Instead, he gave them a lesson about volcanoes. He explained that the Earth was like a big ball of candy, with different layers. The outer shell was the crust, and it was about eighteen miles thick. Underneath was an ocean of fiery, molten rock. In some spots, there were cracks in the crust, and that's where volcanoes formed.

Jess was shocked to learn that there were fifteen hundred volcanoes around the world that could be active. And fourteen of them were right in the Cascades.

How did she not know any of this? None of the kids in the class knew.

On the blacktop, nobody wanted to play kickball. They all nervously eyed the mountain, which rose up in the distance. Kids gathered around as Sam repeated Dr. Morales's story of Mount Pelée. He explained about the warning signs — the rotten-egg stench of sulfur gas, the mudslides, and, of course, the pit vipers. He told them about the fiery hurricane wind that swept down the mountain.

The kids listened with wide eyes and slack jaws. This story was way better than the legend of Skeleton Woman.

On Tuesday, Missy saw a garter snake slithering through the grass behind the blacktop.

"It's a pit viper!" she shrieked.

Other kids freaked out, too. It took Mr. Daley

the rest of recess to calm them down and to convince them that there were no pit vipers in Washington State — or anywhere in the United States.

Over the next few days, the police set up roadblocks on Spirit Lake Memorial Highway. They wouldn't let anyone within ten miles of the mountain, not even loggers.

The whole town seemed to be holding its breath, waiting for something to happen.

And then, on Friday, something did.

It was near the end of the school day, and Jess was gathering her notebooks for dismissal. Suddenly a loud boom rattled their desks and sent Mr. Daley's coffee mug crashing to the floor.

Twenty-one heads turned and stared out the window.

They had a perfect view of St. Helens rising up over the ridge.

It didn't look peaceful anymore.

Pale gray smoke was gushing out of the top.

"It's erupting!" Sam cried.

CHAPTER 10

But the loud boom and gush of smoke wasn't an eruption, not a real one.

Dr. Morales explained this to them that night, when he stopped by the diner.

Mom was behind the counter, and Jess and the twins were at a booth, munching on French fries and trying to focus on their homework. Mr. Rowan was working late, and Mrs. Rowan was still with the twins' grandmother.

They were happy to see Dr. Morales walk through the door. He'd been working on the

MT.GARIBALDI
CANADA
MT.BAKER
GLACIER PEAK
WA
MT.RAINIER
MT. ADAMS
MT.ST.HELENS
MT.HOOD
MT. JEFFERSON
OR
PACIFIC OCEAN
N
E
W
S

MT
ID
CASCADE
VOLCANOES
THREE
SISTERS
NEWBERRY
VOLCANO
CRATER LAKE
MEDICINE LAKE
VOLCANO
MT.SHASTA
CA
LASSEN
PEAK
N

mountain all day, and was heading back to his lab in Seattle.

"I had to come by for another piece of that coconut cake," he said.

Mom and Jess and the twins joined him in a booth, and he explained that what they'd seen and heard from their classroom earlier was called a steam explosion.

"And that's all it was, steam, mixed with a little bit of ash."

In a true volcanic eruption, he went on, the smoke is steel gray or black. And it lasts for many hours or days.

The smoke today had billowed up for just a few minutes, and then turned white and disappeared. The mountain had been peaceful ever since.

"A steam eruption is like a volcano burp," he said.

They all laughed. But Dr. Morales wasn't totally joking.

"It's another warning sign. Nobody should doubt that St. Helens is wide-awake and getting ready to erupt."

There were more steam explosions as the weeks passed. Some lasted for hours. St. Helens was front-page news every day. Some nights Dr. Morales was actually on the TV news, giving updates along with other scientists who were closely studying the mountain.

The twins went bonkers every time Dr. Morales's familiar face popped onto the screen.

"There he is! There he is!" they'd shout.

But for Jess it was better to see Dr. Morales in person, and her heart always leaped a little when he appeared at Clive's. He came in once or twice a week, on his way to or from the mountain. Mom would pile a plate high with his favorite fried chicken or homemade noodles. And between bites of food and sips of coffee, he'd tell them about his work on the mountain.

To Jess and the boys, his stories were like scenes out of a thrilling action movie. A helicopter pilot would fly him up to the top of the volcano — the summit. Those steam explosions had blasted through hundreds of feet of rock and ice. There was now a huge crater on the summit. It was thousands of feet wide and hundreds of feet deep. The helicopter would hover above the summit, and Dr. Morales would hop out. He'd scoop up ash from the crater and gather samples of the gas seeping out.

"You actually go into the crater?" Eddie asked in astonishment.

"I go to the edge," Dr. Morales said. "I can only stay for a few seconds because it's so hot. And I have to get away quickly because if a steam explosion happens while I'm there . . . well . . ."

"You'd be toast," Sam said.

"Sammy!" Mom scolded.

But Dr. Morales laughed. "Actually, I'd be boiled," he said, picking up a floppy yellow noodle. "I'd end up looking something like this."

Of course the twins loved that. Sam told the kids at school all about it on the blacktop the next day.

Missy looked like she might vomit.

But as the weeks passed, Dr. Morales often seemed troubled when he came into the diner.

He was still his warm and friendly self. But he looked weary. Studying an active volcano wasn't all helicopter rides and daredevil stunts. There were endless hours of sitting around and watching for changes. There were nights trying to sleep in a freezing tent, with 30-mile-per-hour winds ripping at the sides.

And there was the frustration of not having any clear answers.

Dr. Morales and the other scientists knew that something was happening inside the volcano. There were many warning signs. That big crater on the summit was growing. There were massive cracks and bulges on the north side of the mountain. But none of the scientists knew for sure what exactly these clues meant.

Was the volcano about to erupt?

Would the eruption be violent?

Would there be a warning?

"We just don't know for sure," Dr. Morales said.

Meanwhile, the mountain quieted down. And some folks in Cedar started to question whether the mountain was really going to erupt after all.

Even some scientists admitted that it was possible that St. Helens could go back to sleep.

At Clive's, people grumbled. Loggers were impatient to get back to work. Cabin owners wanted to check their properties. Fishermen were itching to get back to their favorite streams.

By the middle of May, the steam explosions had stopped. More and more people were becoming convinced that the danger had passed. On the blacktop, kids got tired of talking about the volcano. Missy even started up about Skeleton Woman again.

One day Jess and the boys were tossing a ball around, when Missy came stamping up to Jess.

"You know, I never saw the proof."

"Proof of what?" Jess asked.

"Skeleton Woman's shack," she said, crossing her arms.

Jess rolled her eyes, and the twins groaned.

Not this again.

Of course she and the twins had told all the kids about being in the cabin when the earthquake happened.

"There was nothing there," Eddie snapped.

"But you promised you'd take a picture," Missy said.

"She tried," Sam said.

Eddie and Sam started bickering with Missy.

But Jess was no longer listening.

Because all she could think of now was Dad's camera.

With all of the excitement over the mountain, Jess had managed to keep her mind off the fact that she'd lost Dad's prized possession. She hadn't even told Mom yet.

How could she have been so stupid? Why had she brought Dad's camera into the forest? What would Mom say when she realized it was missing?

Tears flooded Jess's eyes.

She turned and ran off the blacktop, to a quiet spot behind the jungle gym.

Sam and Eddie came to find her.

"What's wrong?" Sam said.

Jess kept her head down so her hair would hide her tears.

"That Missy," Eddie fumed.

"No," Jess choked, wiping her face. "It's not her. It's my dad's camera. I just can't believe I lost it. My mom is going to be so upset."

Dad's camera wasn't just an expensive piece of equipment. It was a part of Dad.

And now it was lying in the dirt in that leaky cabin.

"We'll go find it," Sam said.

"We will," Eddie said.

"How?" Jess said.

The twins looked thoughtful.

"We'll figure out a way," Eddie said.

Then he held out his hand.

Sam put his on top.

Jess hesitated. But then she put her hand on top of Sam's.

They leaned together so that their foreheads were touching.

"All for one," Eddie and Sam chorused.

Jess took a breath.

"And one for all," she answered. And when she felt ready, they walked together back to the blacktop.

CHAPTER 11

THE NEXT MORNING
SATURDAY, MAY 17, 1980
10:00 A.M.
CLIVE'S DINER

Their chance to look for the camera came sooner than Jess expected.

The very next day, the twins came to Clive's as the Saturday breakfast rush was ending.

"Hey, gents," Mom called. "Your mom went out of town again?"

"How'd you know?" Sam asked. "She just left."

Mom smirked. "Magic."

Jess laughed. "It's because you always wear those same disgusting Mariners T-shirts when your mom isn't here to stop you."

The boys looked down at their stained shirts and grinned.

The second Mom went back into the kitchen, the boys pounced on Jess with their news: Their dad was heading up to his fishing cabin early tomorrow morning. He'd left his most expensive fishing rod there, and he wanted to bring it home.

"But how's he going to get there?" Jess asked.

The cabin was eight miles from St. Helens. Jess didn't think the police were letting anyone get that close to the mountain.

"My dad talked to the police chief," Eddie said. "The loggers are going back to work on Monday. And the police are even letting people with cabins on Spirit Lake go up there today."

Jess was shocked. Spirit Lake was right at the base of St. Helens, much closer than Loomis Lake.

Jess paused for a minute, thinking about

Dr. Morales. She was pretty positive he wouldn't be in favor of people going close to the mountain. But even he admitted that nobody knew for sure that St. Helens was going to erupt any time soon. And wouldn't there be some kind of warning before a big eruption?

What Jess did know was that here was her chance to get Dad's camera back. And she needed to take it.

"Your dad will let us come?" she asked.

The boys nodded.

Mom would never approve. But Mom didn't have to know because she wouldn't be home tomorrow. She was leaving early in the morning for Vancouver. The twins' grandma was getting out of the hospital, and Mom wanted to help Mrs. Rowan get her settled. Mom had invited Jess to come along. But Jess said she'd stay with the twins.

Jess couldn't believe her luck.

Maybe she'd be able to get Dad's camera and sneak it back into Mom's trunk. And Mom would never have to find out that it had been missing.

The next morning, Mom kissed Jess good-bye at six thirty.

By seven, Jess and the twins were in the back of Mr. Rowan's pickup, rumbling along Spirit Lake Memorial Highway.

There were no police roadblocks, and they made it to Loomis Lake in under an hour.

They got out of the truck, and they all stood in the parking lot for a moment, staring up at the mountain.

"Looks the same as it always does," Mr. Rowan said.

It was true.

They couldn't see any of the cracks or bulges that Dr. Morales had told them about. The mountain's peak sparkled as usual, and its reflection rippled on the surface of Loomis Lake.

"I don't want to stay long," Mr. Rowan told them. "An hour tops. So don't go far."

He'd barely started to walk away when Jess and the twins were sprinting toward the forest. Soon they lost sight of the mountain; the tall trees blocked their view. Not being able to see the mountain made Jess nervous.

But what rattled her most was the quiet.

She heard none of the usual forest sounds — the chirps of birds and skittering of squirrels and chipmunks. The air was strangely still, without even a breath of wind.

The twins were strangely quiet, too. They walked along without their usual baseball chatter. The hike was taking longer than it had last time. The trail was littered with fallen branches and ripped apart by huge holes caused by the earthquake.

With every step, Jess's stomach twisted tighter. They should turn around, she thought. They needed to find Mr. Rowan and go home. This all felt wrong. She was ready to grab the twins and drag them back down the trail.

But then she saw it, up ahead: the shack.

Jess forgot her fear. All she could think of was Dad's camera.

She hurried ahead, leaping over branches and holes. She ran up to the shack and pushed the door open. She searched all around the floor, but the camera wasn't there.

Her heart sank. She'd been sure she would find it lying on the ground.

And then she saw her backpack sitting on the table.

Strange. She was sure she hadn't left it there, all zipped up.

Jess stepped over and unzipped it.

And to her amazement, the camera was tucked inside, carefully wrapped in the plastic bag. She lifted it up and removed it from the plastic.

It was perfect.

The boys came through the door.

"You found it!" Eddie said happily.

But Jess's relief was mixed with confusion.

"How did it get into the backpack?" Jess wondered. "I know I dropped it."

"Someone must have found it," Sam said. "Maybe a logger."

"But nobody has been allowed to come up here," Jess said. "And Missy said the loggers were too scared to come to this part of the forest."

"Maybe *she* did it," Eddie said.

"Missy?" Jess said.

"No," Eddie said, raising his eyebrows.

"You know . . ."

"You dope," Sam laughed. "Skeleton Woman didn't find Jess's camera and put it in the bag." He grabbed Jess. "Come on. We need to go. Dad will be waiting for us."

Jess put the backpack on and followed the twins out of the cabin.

They'd just stepped outside when Jess caught a whiff of a nasty smell.

The boys smelled it, too.

"Eddie!" Sam chided. "What did you do?"

"It wasn't me!" Eddie said, putting his hands over his face.

They looked at Jess.

"I didn't do it!"

"Ugh," Eddie said. "It's like rotten eggs."

Jess's heart stopped.

"Isn't that what sulfur gas smells like?" she asked.

Sulfur gas. Like on Mount Pelée.

It was one of the warning signs, just before Pelée erupted.

"Is it coming from the mountain?" Eddie asked.

The horrifying answer came a second later.

Kaboom!

CHAPTER 12

SUNDAY, MAY 18
8:32 A.M.

The blast seemed to shatter the sky.

A huge black cloud shot up over the tree line.

Jess's legs turned to jelly.

"That's just a steam explosion, right?" Sam asked weakly.

But they all knew it wasn't.

This angry black cloud looked nothing like the wispy gray plumes they'd seen from Cedar. It boiled wildly and spread out all around until it had painted the entire sky a furious black.

There was a loud *whoosh* that shook the ground.

A blast of searing hot wind knocked them off their feet. The air seemed to turn to fire. Jess had never felt such heat.

It was hotter than the diner kitchen on a broiling August day. Hotter than Mom's oven when she baked bread.

The pyroclastic surge, Jess realized, the fiery hurricane wind packed with poisonous gas and ash.

It was the killer wind that had destroyed Saint-Pierre.

The heat blasted over them, and Jess felt as though she was being cooked from the inside out. Every breath was like inhaling fire.

She looked around with desperation, knowing that they wouldn't last more than a few seconds if they stood here. Just a few yards away was a huge hole, one of the grave-like pits caused by the earthquake. It was wide, and at least ten feet deep.

Almost without thinking, Jess grabbed hold of the twins, gripping their arms with all her might.

"There!" she cried, yanking them toward the huge pit.

It was their only hope.

They all jumped in. Jess came down hard on her shoulder. She bit her tongue and tasted blood.

But she barely noticed.

There was only heat. Terrible, blistering heat.

"Get into the dirt!" Jess screamed.

They all dug frantically into the sides of the hole, trying to tunnel in.

Jess tore at the earth until her fingers were bleeding, until she'd created enough space for her head and shoulders. She jammed herself in, and then pulled her legs to her chest so she was a little ball pushed into the dirt.

The air grew hotter, until she was sure the entire world had burst into flames.

The volcano thundered and roared.

Dirt and mud and bits of rock rained down.

There were terrible moaning shrieks of trees falling above. Jess thought of her great-grandfather Clive. No wonder he'd hated that sound.

Jess kept herself pushed into the dirt. But it was very hard to breathe. Finally the air started to cool down. Jess uncurled her body and stood in the hole. But she had barely taken a breath when a tree came crashing down over the hole.

Bam!

A branch smacked her in the head.

And then there was no more heat, no more pain.

Just darkness.

CHAPTER 13

10 MINUTES LATER

Jess opened her eyes, but she couldn't see.

She brushed the dirt from her eyes and blinked, but there was still only darkness.

Was it night?

Had she gone blind?

Jess sat up, gasping at the searing pain that raked across her back. She'd been badly burned, she could tell.

It took a moment for her mind to clear. And

slowly she grasped the full horror of what was happening.

St. Helens was erupting.

The smoke had turned the day black.

The pyroclastic surge had exploded over them.

Somehow they were still alive in this hole in the ground.

"Sam?" she choked. "Eddie?"

A voice rasped from somewhere close.

"I'm here," Sam said softly. "Eddie's hurt."

Jess inched over, groping in the darkness until her fingers brushed their faces. She felt tears.

Jess fought back her own tears and took a deep breath.

She tried to stand, but the fallen tree imprisoned them in the hole. It would be impossible to try to climb out in the dark. They'd have to wait here until the sky lightened.

But when would that be?

The mountain roared. Every few minutes, there was a new explosion that rattled Jess's bones. Jess couldn't control her fear. She finally started to cry, but luckily the mountain drowned out the sound.

Jess felt something falling on her head, warm flakes.

Ash, she realized.

It began as a few sprinkles, falling lightly like hot snow. And then, suddenly, they were in an ash blizzard. The warm flakes swirled up Jess's nose and into her mouth. She covered her face, but it did no good. The flakes completely filled the air.

The ash tasted disgusting, like dirt mixed with chalk. It clogged up her nose and blocked off her throat. She coughed hard and blew her nose and spit out mouthfuls. But it was coming down too quickly. She couldn't clear her nose and mouth fast enough.

The boys hacked and gagged, too.

They would all suffocate if this kept up.

Then Jess had an idea.

"Pull your shirt over your face!" she cried.

Jess reached below her red sweatshirt for her T-shirt. She pulled it up over her face. It worked! The shirt became a mask that filtered out the ash.

She could breathe again.

They sat in the pit with their faces covered for a long time, waiting for the blizzard to stop. The mountain growled and boomed.

Jess huddled close to the boys.

She realized that there could be only one thing worse than being in the middle of this horror.

Being here alone, without the twins.

CHAPTER 14

ONE HOUR LATER

At last the ash blizzard stopped.

A thick coating of the warm flakes covered their heads and shoulders.

Jess spit and coughed and wiped her eyes.

The sky had lightened up. Finally she could see well enough to climb through the tangle of limbs that covered the hole.

She made her way up until she was high enough to see the forest.

Except it was no longer a forest.

It was a graveyard of fallen trees.

Every single tree was down — thousands and thousands of trees. The force of the blast and the surge had ripped most of them right out of the ground. Two-hundred-foot trees, knocked over like Popsicle sticks.

Some had been uprooted, others snapped like twigs. If Jess and the twins hadn't been deep in that hole, they all would have been crushed.

The cabin was smashed under a huge fir tree.

Everything was covered with a thick coating of gray ash.

But there was a sight even worse than the ruined forest: the mountain.

With the trees down, Jess now had a perfect view of St. Helens.

Or what was left of St. Helens.

It looked as though it had been smashed by a giant hammer. Its sparkling peak was gone. In its place was a gaping black mouth vomiting up smoke.

Jess had never seen anything so hideous.

She slammed her eyes shut and turned away. She climbed back down into the hole again.

And now she could finally really see the boys. Their faces were plastered white with ash and smeared with blood. They looked like two battered ghosts.

Sam was staring down. Jess followed his gaze to his thigh. His pants were torn. What was that on his leg? It didn't look like skin. It looked ripped up and blackened, like burned meat.

Jess gasped.

"Oh, Sam!"

And then she looked at Eddie. She couldn't see his wounds. But from the glazed look in his eyes, she could see that he was badly hurt, too. Both boys were shivering.

They needed to find help — now.

But how? The boys couldn't stand. And Jess wouldn't be able to carry even one of them out.

It was hopeless. They would have to sit here and wait for help to come.

Jess looked up, praying that she'd see Mr. Rowan peering down into the hole. But how would he get to them? It would take hours — even days — for anyone to make it through the maze of fallen trees.

Jess had to get help.

But what if there was another eruption?

What if another fiery hurricane swept over the forest?

What if she got lost?

A hundred terrible questions swirled through her mind, and none had answers.

But that didn't matter, Jess realized.

"I'm going to get help," she said, fighting back tears. "I'll be back very soon."

The boys didn't seem to hear her. Both seemed to be drifting away. Sam's eyes were closed. He was shivering harder now.

Jess gently took Sam's cold hand and laid it on her palm. She lifted Eddie's and put it on top of Sam's. She rested her other hand on top of Eddie's. She gripped both boys' hands tightly within her own.

All for one, she said to herself. *And one for all*.

For the first time, Jess really understood what those words meant.

Jess would do anything to help the boys.

She would even face the volcano by herself.

CHAPTER 15

But which way should she go?

Jess looked around, trying to understand where she was. The trail was gone. Nothing looked familiar. It was as though she'd crash-landed on a distant planet, a smoking, ash-covered land.

The only landmarks were the smashed shack and the mountain. Dad had taught her to use the sun as a guide. But the sun was blotted out by the ash and smoke.

Jess decided that if she walked with the volcano on her left, she should at least be heading back toward the parking lot. Then maybe she could find Mr. Rowan. If she couldn't, at least she'd be close to the road. It was so hot that her clothes were sticking to her sweat-soaked skin. Jess stripped off her sweatshirt and dropped it over a branch. Then she took a breath and set out.

She walked between fallen trees, and when there was no room between the trees, she climbed up and walked along their trunks. Everything was covered with inches of ash, and in some spots it was very hot. The air smelled like rotten eggs and smoke. Her back throbbed with pain.

But even worse was the thirst. Her lips were cracked and bleeding, her tongue swollen and sandpaper dry. She hadn't had a sip of water since she'd left home. How long ago was that?

Just this morning, this forest had been crisscrossed by creeks filled with clear rushing water. On her camping trips with Dad, they'd scooped up water right from streams and gulped it down without a worry. But now every stream she passed was ruined. The ash had turned the sparkling water to thick gray sludge that stank of sulfur. Just the thought of trying to swallow a mouthful was nauseating.

The sounds of the volcano pounded in her ears. It roared. It thundered. It boomed. Bolts of lightning shot through the churning cloud above. Her footsteps kicked up clouds of ash that burned her eyes.

But Jess ignored the pain and the thirst and the volcano's roar. She fought the swirl of terrifying thoughts that screamed through her mind.

Instead she pictured Dad's hopeful eyes. She imagined her great-grandfather Clive Marlowe tramping through these very woods alone when he was just a few years older than Jess.

She tried to hear Mom's voice.

"Whatever happens, you and I will make it through."

But what really kept her feet moving was Sam and Eddie.

Her best friends.

For as long as Jess could remember, they'd been right there with her. In those terrible months after Dad died, the twins had hardly ever left her side. They'd even slept on the floor of her room. She pictured their freckled faces, imagined the feel of their hands.

Jess stumbled along for hours, for miles she was sure. The parking lot was nowhere in sight. She was afraid she might be walking in circles.

And then she came into a big field, a place she'd never seen before. And that's when she realized she was completely lost.

She crouched down on the hot, ashy ground, too exhausted to even cry. Every inch of her body ached. Her lungs burned from the ash. She had never imagined that she could be so thirsty. If only she could sleep for a little while. Everything would be better when she woke up. The sky would be blue again. The mountain would be quiet. All of this would be over.

She let her eyes drift closed. She had the feeling of letting go, of floating away. The pain and thundering noise faded.

No!

She forced herself to stand up.

What was she thinking! She had to keep going. She had to find help for the twins. She could not give up.

And that's when she noticed a new sound.

Not a roar or a boom or a whoosh.

Thwack, thwack, thwack, thwack.

A helicopter.

Jess leaped to her feet and searched the sky.

And there it was: a yellow chopper, flying in circles.

She jumped up and waved.

"Hey! Hey! Here I am!"

But of course they couldn't hear her.

And she was so covered with ash. She was just another speck of gray in the endless ash sea. How would they see her?

The helicopter disappeared. And then it circled back a minute later. Jess jumped up and waved, but it flew away again. The pilot couldn't see her.

What could Jess do? How could she get their attention before they flew away?

And then it came to her.

She found a big branch and snapped off a stick covered with leaves.

She used it to sweep the ground around her, to create a huge cloud of ash that rose up like a smoke signal. And then she ran out in front of it, waving her arms.

The helicopter slowed.

It swooped down a bit and hovered over her.

A man leaned out and waved. He shouted through a bullhorn.

"We're coming down for you!"

A wave of relief almost knocked Jess to the ground.

The *thwack, thwack, thwack, thwack* got louder and louder, until it drowned out the sound of the volcano. The wind from the propeller kicked up so much ash that Jess could barely see. But moments later a man in a bright orange vest appeared out of the cloud. He knelt down.

"You okay?" he shouted.

Jess didn't answer for a second.

But then she nodded. She was okay.

He helped Jess up and started to lead her to the chopper.

"No!" she cried. "I can't leave my friends here! They're hurt! We have to get them!"

"Where are they?"

Jess turned and pointed to the wasteland all around them.

"Somewhere out there!"

"Okay," he said calmly. "Let's get up into the air. You're going to help us find them."

And so, minutes later, Jess was strapped into the backseat of a four-seat helicopter. The pilot was up front, and the man in the vest was next to her. He gave her a thermos of water and big earphones to protect her ears from the engine noise.

She looked out the window, combing the ground with her eyes.

But everything looked the same, ash-covered trees as far as she could see. The air was filled with smoke. It was almost impossible to see anything.

How would they ever spot the twins?

But then Jess saw it — a flash of red.

Her sweatshirt.

Her heart leaped up.

"There!" Jess cried. "There they are!"

The man tapped the pilot's shoulder and pointed down. The helicopter swooped around and headed for the twins.

She had found them.

CHAPTER 16

TWO MONTHS LATER
SUNDAY, JULY 20, 1980
SEATTLE, WASHINGTON

Jess was cleaning up her room.

She checked the clock.

Ten o'clock. Better hurry.

She and Mom were having visitors today, and they'd been working nonstop all weekend to get the apartment ready.

They'd been in their new place for only a week, but already they were unpacked. Jess loved her new room, which was bright and sunny. She was still getting used to the Seattle noises and the crowds of people. But she liked it here more than she'd expected to.

She moved carefully — the burn on her back still hurt if she turned too suddenly. But it had healed well. She was glad she couldn't see what it looked like.

Mom popped her head through the doorway.

"Let's not forget our camera," Mom said.

"I have it ready," Jess said.

Their new camera.

Jess had finally worked up the courage to tell Mom the whole story about losing Dad's camera.

"It was Dad's prized possession," Jess had said, fighting tears.

Mom had put her arms around her.

"No," she'd said. "You were."

Mom looked around Jess's room now and smiled.

"It looks great in here," she said.

Jess agreed.

The walls were covered with photographs of

trees and birds and of Mom — pictures that Dad had taken. His dream had been for his photographs to hang in a Seattle gallery, and now that dream had come true — almost.

"And I really do love the red," Mom said, admiring the freshly painted walls.

Jess loved the color, too. She knew that for the rest of her life, red would be her lucky color.

Dr. Morales had helped them paint the room. Jess was glad to see that their friend was starting to smile again. He'd been safe at his lab here in Seattle when St. Helens erupted. But like many of the scientists, he blamed himself for not being able to better predict the eruption. And he'd lost one of his close friends, a young scientist who had been near the mountain when it exploded.

That man was one of the fifty-seven people who died in the eruption. Some people were killed instantly, in the pyroclastic surge and blast of rock and ash. Others died in the floods and mudslides that raced down the mountain in the hours afterward.

Dr. Morales had been right when he predicted

that Mount St. Helens would erupt with terrible violence. But not even he had imagined just how powerful the eruption would be. It was one of the most powerful in history, more explosive even than Pelée.

The entire front of the mountain shattered. Millions of tons of rock and ice and volcanic debris crashed down the mountain. The pyroclastic surge instantly destroyed everything within its five-mile path. If Jess and the twins had been much closer, they would not have escaped with their lives.

A mudslide swept down the mountain, picking up trees and logs and trucks and houses and bridges. The downtown of Cedar was spared. But some people lost their homes, including Missy. She and her family were with relatives in Iowa now. Jess was thinking about writing to her. She wanted to tell Missy the news: that Skeleton Woman really did exist!

In a way.

Jess had discovered this about a month after the eruption.

By then Jess's burn had mostly healed. She and Mom had been helping serve meals at a shelter for people who had lost their homes. There was another volunteer working that day, an older woman with a long gray braid and bright blue eyes.

"I know you," the woman had said to Jess with a smile.

And Jess remembered her — she was the woman with the white pickup who they'd seen in the Loomis Lake parking lot, the day of that first earthquake.

Her name was Gretchen Livingston. She worked for a group that had been trying to save the big old trees near Loomis Lake.

Gretchen and Mom had hit it off. And a few nights later at Clive's, Gretchen had told Mom and Jess her secret — that she was Skeleton Woman.

"What?" Jess had gasped.

Gretchen smiled slyly.

"For years our group had been trying to find ways to stop the lumber company from chopping down those beautiful old trees," she'd explained. "But nothing we did worked. And finally the company was going to cut them all down. I ready to give up. But one day I was at a restaurant over in Cougar."

That was a town across the valley.

"I overheard some loggers in the booth behind me. They were talking about the old Skeleton Woman legend. Of course I'd heard that story when I was a kid."

"Me too," Mom said.

"The men were spooked by the story. I guess the old witch was supposed to live near Loomis Lake, in that old-growth forest, right where they were supposed to be cutting."

She leaned forward.

"That gave me an idea."

She found out when the cutting of the trees was set to begin. And she snuck up to that part of the forest. She went into the shack and waited.

"I got my hair all wild, and I splattered some red paint on my clothes."

"I saw that paint! In the shack!" Jess said.

"As the men were getting their chain saws ready," Gretchen continued, "I burst out of the cabin. I dashed through the forest very quickly so they would catch just a glimpse of me."

She smiled proudly.

"And that did it. They wouldn't go back."

That's when it dawned on Jess.

"So you're the one who found my camera in the cabin?"

"Ah, that was your camera!" she said. "I couldn't imagine who would have left it there."

"We were looking for Skeleton Woman," Jess said.

"Well, you found her!" Gretchen said.

They all laughed.

Then Gretchen got tears in her eyes.

"But of course the forest is gone now," she said.

Not even Skeleton Woman could stop St. Helens from destroying it all. Two hundred and thirty miles of wilderness had been burned, ripped apart, or buried under a hundred feet of mud and debris. Millions of trees were killed by the burning wind.

"The forest will grow back one day," Mom had said, in her usual hopeful way. "Nature has an amazing power to heal itself."

Dr. Morales had told them that.

And it was true. The trees *would* grow back. The animals *would* return.

But it would take decades.

And Jess wasn't sure she ever wanted to go back.

She wanted to remember her beautiful mountain the way it had been.

It was only a few weeks after that talk that Mom had decided that she was finally ready to move to Seattle. She wanted to go back to college, to become a teacher. She wanted Jess to discover life outside Cedar.

Mr. Rowan had offered to buy Clive's. He'd been badly hurt in the eruption, and didn't want to go back to his regular job. Mr. and Mrs. Rowan would run the restaurant. And of course the twins would help. So, in a way, Clive's would stay in the Marlowe family.

Jess's throat tightened up as she thought of the twins. She would never forget those terrifying hours after they were rescued from the forest. The boys had been flown to a special hospital in

Portland, Oregon, where they stayed for weeks. When they finally got home, Jess slept on the floor of their room every night until they were strong again.

Jess still wasn't used to not seeing them every day. But when she closed her eyes, she could hear their happy, bickering voices. When she felt lonely, she could feel their hands gripping hers in their secret handshake. She'd spoken to them every day since the move. And today the whole Rowan family was coming to visit.

Jess and Mom had a big surprise for the twins: a Mariners game.

A few minutes later, the doorbell rang.

Jess rushed to the door.

She flung it open, and there they were, Sam and Eddie.

Two buzz-cut heads, four smiling green eyes, and ten thousand freckles.

Four strong arms grabbed hold of her.

Three hearts pounded with happiness.

It was a long time before they let each other go.

WHY I TOOK SO LONG TO CREATE A GIRL MAIN CHARACTER

I have featured some amazing girls in many of my I Survived books, like Zena, who helped her brother, Max, escape from the Nazis, and Jennie, who led Oscar and her brother, Bruno, through the blazing streets of Chicago during the Great Fire of 1871. But I had never put a girl on the cover. I always told the stories through the eyes of a boy.

The reason for this is that I have three boys of my own (Leo, Jeremy, and Dylan). And none of them liked to read. It was very hard for them to find books that they really loved. I could rarely convince them to read a book that had a girl main character.

And so about six years ago, I decided to write a few books that I thought my own boys would really like. I thought of the title I Survived, and imagined a series of four books featuring boys going through disasters from history.

I had already written two other books, both about a girl named Emma-Jean Lazarus. I thought the whole I Survived project would take about a year, and then I'd get back to my beloved Emma-Jean.

But four I Survived books turned into six, which became eight, then twelve, and on and on. It so happened that not only boys liked the books, but girls, too. This made me very happy. And then some of those girls started to write to me.

Girls like Amelia: "Mrs. Tarshis, why are there no girls on your covers?" And Chloe: "I don't understand why there aren't any girl main characters." And Maya, and Charlotte, and Mariella . . . and hundreds of others.

I would write back to each of them to explain about my boys. I told them that it always seemed to me that there were more books for girls like my own daughter, Valerie, than for boys like my sons. I told them about the thousands of boys (and their teachers and parents) who have written to me to say that they never liked to read, and that the I Survived books inspired them to become readers.

But the girls kept writing to me, too, and some emails were a little angry.

"Don't you think girls are strong, too?" wrote Matty.

"What about us?" wrote Ali and Elena.

So after long talks with my editor, Nan, I decided that it really didn't matter if my character was a boy or a girl. I decided that those devoted boy readers of I Survived probably wouldn't care if the main character was a girl or a boy — as long as the books were exciting and interesting.

And guess what? The writing experience for this book was no different from the others. My

I Survived books are so hard to write! Creating Jess was just as difficult for me as creating Max and Oscar and the other boys of I Survived. I love her just as much.

And really, my books are not about boys or girls, are they? They're about young people who go through difficult and frightening experiences and discover their inner strength. They're about how people can find inspiration and comfort from their family and friends and their faith. The I Survived books are not boy books or girl books. They are, I hope, human books.

And to Amelia, Chloe, Maya, Charlotte, Mariella, Matty, Ali, Elena, and the many hundreds of girls who have written to me, I am truly sorry it took me so long!

QUESTIONS AND ANSWERS ABOUT THE ERUPTION OF MOUNT ST. HELENS

Why did I write about the eruption of Mount St. Helens?

The eruption of Mount St. Helens in 1980 was one of the most environmentally destructive in world history. It was the most powerful natural disaster ever recorded in America, more powerful than Hurricane Katrina in 2005 or the San Francisco Earthquake of 1906.

And yet many people under the age of thirty have barely even heard of it. How can that be?

We tend to remember disasters that result in large numbers of human deaths. The St. Helens eruption destroyed 230 miles of wilderness. But because the mountain was surrounded mostly by forests, it claimed far fewer lives than many other destructive volcanoes. Fifty-seven people died in St. Helens. More "famous" volcanoes like Vesuvius and Krakatoa killed tens of thousands.

But the eruption of St. Helens was very important, and not just because it happened right here in the United States. It was the first volcano that scientists could study closely while it was revving up for its eruption. Today, volcano scientists (called volcanologists) have a much better understanding of volcanoes than they did in 1980. And that is because of the lessons learned from St. Helens.

What happened when St. Helens erupted?

On the morning of May 18, Mount St. Helens erupted with the force of a one-megaton nuclear bomb, which is equal to ten million tons of dynamite. The front of the mountain actually shattered apart and collapsed with rocks tumbling down the mountain in a massive avalanche. The explosion created a cloud of ash, smoke, and gas that shot more than twelve miles up into the sky. It triggered one of history's biggest landslides. It was fifty miles wide. The wave of mud and debris and melted ice raced down the mountain and swept away bridges, thousands of trees and logs, cars, houses, bulldozers, and roads.

The eruption spewed a staggering amount of ash — 520 million tons of it. The ash blew eastward, across the United States. In the city of Spokane, Washington, 350 miles away, the ash caused complete darkness. As far away as Montana, ash from St. Helens ruined crops, caused car accidents, and clogged airplane engines.

Did the eruption really take people by surprise?

Yes, the eruption was a surprise, and to me, that was the most incredible part of the story. There were so many warning signs — thousands of earthquakes (yes, *thousands*) between March 20 and the eruption on May 18. There were dozens of steam explosions, some that lasted for hours.

Huge cracks formed in the mountain. Near the summit, the mountain was actually bulging out from the pressure inside it. Just two years before, two scientists wrote a research paper warning that St. Helens was likely to erupt in the coming years.

And yet, the eruption on the morning of May 18 was a true surprise, even to scientists. The mountain had quieted down in the weeks right before. Most scientists had thought there would be some very dramatic warning before it exploded. But that warning never came. One minute the mountain was peaceful, and the next it erupted with a violence that few had imagined.

Are scientists better able to predict eruptions today?

Yes. Today scientists have far better tools for studying volcanoes. They have computer programs that can analyze huge amounts of data in seconds. They have lasers that can detect whether melted rock — magma — is rising up through the volcano.

But what truly changed volcano science was the eruption of Mount St. Helens. Scientists from all around the world have studied every second of that eruption. This work has helped scientists better understand the warning signs that often lead to volcanic eruptions.

Could St. Helens erupt again?

Yes. In fact, it already has many times since 1980. Some of the eruptions have released huge clouds of ash into the sky. In 2004, it spewed 26 billion gallons of lava. (How did they measure that? I wish I knew!) But none has come close to the fury of the 1980 eruption.

What are the world's most dangerous volcanoes?

There are 1,500 volcanoes in the world that could be active, from the lava-spewing Kilauea of Hawaii to the steaming Katla of Iceland to the quietly beautiful Mount Fuji in Japan.

About 160 of the world's most active volcanoes are located in a horseshoe-shaped area surrounding the Pacific Ocean. This area is called the Ring of Fire.

The Cascade mountain range, where St. Helens is located, is part of this ring.

Any active volcano is dangerous. But what makes a volcano perilous to humans is mainly its location. Volcanoes located near big cities are far more dangerous than those in remote areas. The eruption of Mount St. Helens could have killed thousands if it had been near a more crowded area.

And here are some more intriguing facts I found about Mount St. Helens:

Height of eruption cloud: The main volcanic cloud rose to between 12 and 15 miles into the sky, into the Earth's stratosphere.

Number of earthquakes before eruption: More than 2,000

Area destroyed by eruption: About 230 square miles (more than three times the size of Washington, DC)

Size of landslide: 23 square miles

Depth of landslide: Roughly 100 feet

Speed of landslide: 70–150 miles per hour

Distance traveled by ash cloud: Ash could have circled the globe three times; small amounts of ash fell over 22,200 square miles.

Height of St. Helens before eruption: 9,677 feet (It was the fifth-tallest mountain in the Cascades.)

Height after eruption: 8,363 feet (It is now the fourteenth tallest.)

Number of bridges destroyed: 27

Miles of highway destroyed: 185

Number of trees destroyed: Roughly 3 million

FOR FURTHER READING AND LEARNING

Check out these great books to learn more about Mount St. Helens and volcanoes.

Eruption!: Volcanoes and the Science of Saving Lives, by Elizabeth Rusch, New York: Houghton Mifflin Books for Children, 2013

I loved this fascinating book about volcano scientists who used their knowledge and experience from St. Helens to predict an eruption on Mount Pinatubo, in the Philippines, in 1991.

Footprints in the Ash: The Explosive Story of Mount St. Helens, by John Morris and Steven A. Austin, Green Forest, AR: Master Books, 2003

Packed with amazing photographs and maps, this book is fun to read and it takes you deep into the science of volcanoes.

Volcano: The Eruption and Healing of Mount St. Helens, by Patricia Lauber, New York: Simon and Schuster, 1986

This is a great overview of the eruption that gives you a real sense of what the mountain was like before, during, and after.

My book *I Survived the Destruction of Pompeii, AD 79*, focuses on the eruption of Mount Vesuvius, in Italy, which happened nearly 2,000 years ago. I was fascinated by the similarities and differences between these two historic disasters.

I SURVIVED HISTORIANS CLUB

HC

Go behind the scenes of the I SURVIVED series with Lauren Tarshis!

- Read Lauren's blog posts about her research and writing.

- See historical photos and learn facts about the I SURVIVED events.

- Chat with Lauren and other club members on the message boards.

www.scholastic.com/isurvived